Speeding Star
an imprint of
Enslow Publishers, Inc.

ZOMBIE
ZAPPERS
by Nadia Higgins
Book 2

GOT

TO PATRICIA, FOR A GREAT IDEA AND FOR THINKING I COULD DO IT -- NH

Library of Congress Cataloging-in-Publication Data

Higgins, Nadia.
  Zombie field day / Nadia Higgins.
     p. cm. — (Zombie Zappers ; bk. 2)
  Summary: "Join the Zombie Zappers back at school for the next round of zombie mayhem. When Rotfield Middle School students start turning into zombies, Leo and his friends are the only ones who might be able to save them. Can they discover the cause of this outbreak before it's too late?"— Provided by publisher.
  ISBN 978-1-62285-005-1
  [1. Zombies—Fiction. 2. Middle schools—Fiction. 3. Schools—Fiction.] I. Title.
  PZ7.H5349558Zof 2013
  [Fic]—dc23
               2012028662

Future editions:
Paperback ISBN: 978-1-62285-006-8   EPUB ISBN: 978-1-62285-008-2
Single-User PDF ISBN: 978-1-62285-009-9   Multi-User PDF ISBN: 978-1-62285-144-7

Printed in the United States of America

042013 Lake Book Manufacturing, Inc., Melrose Park, IL

10 9 8 7 6 5 4 3 2 1

To Our Readers:
We have done our best to make sure all Internet addresses in this book were active and appropriate when we went to press. However, the author and the Publisher have no control over, and assume no liability for, the material available on those Internet sites or on other Web sites they may link to. Any comments or suggestions can be sent by e-mail to comments@speedingstar.com or to the address below.

Speeding Star
Box 398, 40 Industrial Road
Berkeley Heights, NJ 07922
USA
www.speedingstar.com

Cover Illustration: Daryll Collins

Table of Contents

1

ZOMBIEZAPPER #1

Leo yawned and rubbed his eyes. He squinted at his alarm clock until the red blur turned into numbers. He had time to fit in a quick update before school. His laptop was still open on his legs from last night. Leo pressed a button, and the familiar screen of his Web site lit up.

For all your zombie needs, the slogan read. Hmmm. Maybe he needed something catchier. No time to think about that now, though. Leo scrolled over to the "Z-News" section and started typing:

Good morning, zombie geeks! ZombieZapper #1 here with an update. Yes, folks, this is a true story. It's my own report from the field. My assistants and I are still sorting through the data. But I can tell you this: Z-spotting at Rotfield Mall confirmed yesterday at 12:06 p.m.

Location: In-Between Burger.

Subject: Teenage male, light brown hair, blue eyes.

Skin color: Gray!

- *Clue #1: When I asked for extra ketchup, he just groaned and pointed at a tub of relish.*

- *Clue #2: Definite zombie halitosis (i.e., breath smelled like fuzzy cheese).*

- *Clue #3: Fingernail fell off while he counted my change. Zombie geeks, I cannot stress enough. Caution!*

"ZombieZapper. . . . Seriously?"

Leo slammed his laptop shut. His stepsister Shelly was smirking over his shoulder.

"Shelly, what the—? Get out!" Leo sputtered. He tried to untangle himself from the mess of blankets.

"Leo, you're late." She tapped her watch with a sparkly fingernail. "I had *planned* to get to school early to organize my locker." Hands on hips, Shelly took in the sight of her stepbrother flailing under his zombie-themed comforter.

Leo finally plopped onto the floor, dragging the sheets with him. When he looked up at Shelly, she had that determined look she got before she had to do something unpleasant. Like flushing a dead fish or cleaning up dog poop.

"Leo, you look like a troll. Did you even sleep last night? Leo—ooooh, gross." Shelly felt something slippery under her foot. She bent down and picked up a plastic baggie with two fingernail tips. She peered at the bright green blob in the bottom. "Leo, is this a *slug*?"

"Gimme that." Leo grabbed the bag. "It's a sample. For science."

"You mean for your zombie stuff?" Shelly's voice was the opposite of impressed.

"I mean for zombie *science*," Leo said. "This slug is a decomposer. It's important to stage four of the zombie life cycle."

"Don't you mean *death* cycle?" Shelly was in the doorway now. She had her trying-to-be-patient look.

"Okay, technically—" Leo began.

"Seriously, Leo. Sweetie." Shelly cut him off. Leo *hated* when she acted like his mother just because she was in seventh grade and he was in sixth. "Don't you think it's time to lay off the zombie stuff just a bit? Leo, I'm worried about you."

Gag. "I'm FINE." Leo got up and shut the door behind his stepsister. He listened to her click-click down the stairs. Even her footsteps sounded in charge.

"I bet I'd like you better as a zombie," Leo said under his breath. Then he shook his slug out of the bag. He carefully slid it into a jar with air holes and a rotting finger.

CHAPTER

2

ZOMBIE ALERT

"Roger?" Leo called softly into his open closet. He kicked a mound of dirty underwear to the side and waded through a pile of notebooks. "Roger?" He held out the jar in front of him. "Do you have a second?"

With a *whoosh*, the back of Leo's closet slid open to reveal Roger's smiling green face. "My dear boy, what do I have but an endless *stream* of seconds?" Roger was using his fake British accent again.

Leo smiled. "Roger, you've got to be the weirdest zombie on the planet."

"Half-zombie," Roger corrected him.

Of course. How could Leo forget? Roger was touchy about his zombie status. As Roger liked to explain, he had barely escaped the zombie attack that wiped out his town back in second grade. He was not *bitten* by the zombie who'd infected him—only licked.

After that came what Roger called the "unspeakable time." His parents and both his brothers had been *fully* bitten. Leaving home was the only way Roger could protect his human side. He drifted from town to town for a while. But then Roger got lonely. He started joining Leo's T-ball games at the Rotfield Rec Center. Back then, Leo didn't know anything about zombies. But he noticed that Roger seemed even slower than a regular slow kid at T-ball. And a bit greener too.

Then Roger's ear got blown off by the wind at third base. Leo was the only one who noticed. But he didn't freak out. Instead, he brought Roger home and helped glue the ear back on. That day, Leo became a zombie scientist.

Roger's experience as a half-zombie was a huge help. "My heart still beats at least once an hour," he would say while Leo took notes. "That slows the rotting process quite a bit."

It was true. With glue, Band-Aids, and a few fake teeth, Roger *might* have been able to pass as a human. But what if somebody found out? Or what if Roger's nose got blown off and lost forever? Or a dog bit him and became a half-zombie too? It was too risky.

For now, the two friends agreed the best place for Roger was working in their hidden zombie lab. Roger barely ever needed to sleep, eat, or go to the bathroom. The small, cluttered room they had built in the back of Leo's closet served his half-zombie needs well.

A tower of machines hummed, beeped, and blinked along one wall of the lab. Shelves along another wall held rows of fizzing tubes and bubbling beakers. Above those were tangles of plants and herbs. Rubber gloves, droppers, lab coats, microscope parts, and jars of pills and powders oozed from a cabinet in the corner.

It was no wonder the lab was so stuffed. The two friends had been adding to it for more than four years now. Leo and his best (100% human) friend, Chad, had recently added a merchandise section to Leo's Zombie Zappers Web site. Chad's homemade zombie T-shirts were selling so fast Chad could barely keep them in stock. Now they could afford supplies whenever they needed them.

Roger plopped down on a box labeled "Caution: Hazardous Materials." "How's my finger?" he asked. He waved a four-fingered hand toward the jar Leo was holding. "Any luck with the *Mucinus maximus*?"

"Nothing so far," Leo said. He handed the jar to Roger. The bright green slug was curled up on Roger's middle knuckle. "The skin on the finger might turn purple before it turns pink," Leo added. "That's what I read online."

"Roger that," Roger said, grinning.

Leo groaned. "You seriously are the weirdest zombie ever." He stepped back into the closet to leave and slipped on the pile of notebooks.

"Half-zombie!" Roger said. He pulled Leo up by an elbow.

"Half-zombie," Leo repeated. Then he took off for school, late as usual.

Leo slid into his seat right as the morning bell rang. Chad flashed his notebook at Leo from across the aisle. "Will you be mine?" it said. Chad ran a finger across his chubby chest. He was wearing one of his recent T-shirt creations. This one showed a heart (a real one) dripping gore onto the words, "Be My Zalentine."

That made Leo snort out loud. Chad added a fake burp. Leo looked over at Mandy Wagner to his left. This was when she'd normally roll her eyes and say, "Nice." Or she might shove her desk over an inch with a huff.

But Mandy wasn't even looking at them. She just stared ahead. Leo waved his hands in front of her face. "Helllooooo?" Mandy didn't even blink. A pencil slowly rolled between her feet.

Leo gave Chad a look that said, "What's up with her?" Chad shrugged, "Who knows?" and pointed at Josiah Sullivan behind him. Josiah had the same look as Mandy, only a line of drool dripped down his chin.

"Z-alert???" Chad held up his notebook again.

Leo felt tingly all over. Could it be? Were his classmates turning into zombies right before his eyes? Leo recorded more strange stuff in his notebook as the day went on:

- *10:20. Media. Mrs. Snyder stares at blank computer screen for whole class. DOES NOT BLINK ONCE.*

- *12:45. P.E., swimming pool. Molly Fisher floats FACE DOWN for 45 minutes. Mr. Brown pulls her out of the pool by one leg. She barfs green water and walks away.*

- *1:01. Math. Maddie Lee turns her head in my direction. Must be zombie. NO OTHER POSSIBLE EXPLANATION!*

"What are we going to do?" Chad whispered to Leo as the two friends passed on the way to their reading groups at 2:03.

"I don't know," Leo admitted. "I mean, they're not biting, at least not yet. Did you see any attacks?"

"Attacks of creepiness," Chad said. "Did you see that stuff coming out of Jeremy Berry's ear?"

"I need to talk to Roger," Leo said. "He can help us figure out what's happening. But for now, we need to protect as many people as possible. It's time for Operation Zombie Code. Meet me by the flagpole at 3:13."

CHAPTER

3

OPERATION ZOMBIE CODE

L eo knew he was a zombie expert. But outside the lab, he didn't like getting his hands dirty. And for that matter, he really hated talking to adults. Or talking to kids he didn't know. Or talking to a group of kids. And those skills were exactly what Operation Zombie Code required. This was where Chad came in handy.

"So here's what you have to read." Leo handed Chad a sheet of paper. "But first we have to get Principal VanSchlossen's permission."

"I'll win him over with a sick armpit fart." Chad pumped his hand inside his T-shirt to demonstrate.

"This is serious, Chad. Principal V barely ever lets kids do morning announcements."

"But nobody can resist the charms of The Chad. Check it out." Chad held out the paper and read aloud in his deepest voice:

"Fellow Students and Staff of Rotfield Middle School: You may be in serious danger. A zombie virus is likely spreading within our school walls. Do not panic! The source is yet to be known. In the meantime, protect yourself by following the Three-Point Zombie Code of Conduct.

"Rule #1: Do not touch anyone. No hugs, no high fives, no tagging, nothing.

"Rule #2: Do not make loud noises. This could trigger a zombie attack.

"Rule #3: Do not eat strange food. This includes school food.

"Thank you in advance for your cooperation. Stay tuned for updates from your zombie research team, Leo Wiley and Chad Romero."

"Perfect!" Leo said. "Now comes the hard part."

"No prob," Chad said. He was already leading the way to the principal's office. Leo could suddenly feel his intestines squeezing the ham sandwich he'd had for lunch.

Principal V's door had a smoky white glass window. In an arc across the top of the window were gold capital letters that said, "EVIL GENIUS AT WORK."

"Ooooh," Leo groaned. He leaned against the wall and hugged his stomach.

"It's just a joke," Chad said. He stood on his toes to peek through the window. "He's at his desk." And before Leo could get more nervous, Chad was pounding on the glass.

The door creaked open slightly. "Who goes there?" The principal had clearly been in the middle of something. He glared down at them through tiny square glasses on the tip of his nose. A black rubber band kept the glasses on tight. It stretched around his fluffy ball of hair and dented the middle so his head looked like a fuzzy gray mushroom. He was wearing spotless white gloves. White cloths hung from his belt like a hula skirt.

"What do you want?" He spat a fine mist that sparkled on Chad's curly brown hair.

Chad began, "Sir, we're here because—"

"How dare you interrupt me when I am doing my *work*?" the principal said with a huffy breath. After a moment, he opened the door wide with one foot and waved them gruffly into his office.

"Whoa," Leo said. Every wall was lined with narrow shelves from top to bottom. Each shelf held a long row of perfectly spaced pointy objects. And under each object was a number.

"What are *those*?" Chad whispered to Leo. He thought he could make out a white horse—a unicorn?—with the number 632 below it. Next to it was—another unicorn? This one had pink hooves. Leo's eyes skipped across the room. Number 32 was, yes, a unicorn—a clear glass one. Next to it was another glass one with a purple horn.

"Obviously," Principal V fake smiled down at them, flashing perfectly white teeth, "I'm far too busy to entertain right now. Can't you see I'm in the middle of dusting the 700s shelf of my miniature unicorn collection?"

"Of course, sir. This will just take one minute." Chad fluttered the paper he was holding. "We'd like to show you our important announcement—"

"What part of *busy* don't you understand?" Principal V hissed, his pink tongue flicking behind his teeth.

"It's just that, sir, it's very important—"

Principal V leaned down and peered straight into Chad's eyes. "What. Is. Your. Name." It was a threat more than a question.

Chad coughed into one hand and took one tiny step backward. For the first time Leo could remember, he saw Chad unsure of what to say.

And just like that, anger swirled inside Leo. It scraped away his queasy fear. He pushed in front of Chad and looked straight into the principal's small, mud-colored eyes.

"I'm Leo Wiley," he shouted. "And we're trying to save the school from a zombie attack!"

"Ahhh-haaa-haaa-ha-haaaa." Principal V's laugh came out in hot, sour blasts. Leo blinked as each one hit his face, but he did not step back.

"Yeah, that's right, zombies!" Chad had recovered from his speechless moment and slung an arm around Leo's shoulder as if for protection.

Principal V stood up to his full height. He smoothed the ring of cloths around his belt. "That's ridiculous," he snarled. "Now get out." He whipped out a cloth and snapped it in the boys' general direction. And with a blast of air, the door slammed in their faces.

CHAPTER

4

BACKUP OPERATION ZOMBIE CODE

"Good news." Chad was sitting in Leo's kitchen. He had tipped back his chair and was licking a Popsicle. Blue lines ran down his chin. He scribbled in a sketchbook. "I have a new idea for a merchandise item." He held up a picture of a baby wearing a bib that said, "Zombie in Training." "Awesome, huh?"

How did Chad do it? Leo wondered. It was like his best friend lived inside an invisible force field that bounced problems away into outer space.

"That's great, Chad," Leo sighed.

"I think it would work on those baby T-shirts that snap under the crotch too."

"It's good," Leo admitted, but he was too worried to talk shop right now. "Chad?"

"Mmmmm-hmmmmm?"

"Backup Operation Zombie Code begins now."

That night, Leo felt a little better. He and Chad had sneaked into the broken second-story window by Room 203. (Chad got in by climbing the dumpster. Then he opened a door for Leo.) They'd hung 175 copies of the Three-Point Zombie Code everywhere except the girls' bathrooms. Leo fell asleep knowing he'd done his duty to protect his fellow students—at least until he could start working on a cure.

The next morning, Leo got to school on time. Or he tried to.

"Are you *kidding* me?!" Shelly screamed in Leo's face before he'd even made it up the school steps. She was holding a bunch of crumpled fliers in her hand. "Did you even think of me before you pulled this stunt? How am I going to live this down?" Was she actually crying? "You're coming with me right now to take these down, Leonard Francis!"

Leo cringed. "Shut up!" he hissed. How could she yell his middle name at school like that? "You should be thanking me for protecting you!"

Shelly grabbed Leo by the wrist. "Look at this!" She kicked the school doors open. "Look at what you've done!"

Leo searched his brain for the right word. What was it? Oh yeah. *Backfired.* Most of the kids were laughing. A lot of them were pretending to be zombies. This included loud moaning and falling on top of each other.

Others were freaking out. This group was hugging and sharing lots of damp Kleenex.

"LEONARD FRANCIS WILEY!" Again with the middle name? Principal V's voice boomed over the intercom. "Report to my office RIGHT THIS SECOND!"

Leo swallowed hard. He looked up at Shelly. Even she looked scared. "You'd better go," she said. Then, maybe to be nice, "I won't tell Dad."

Leo knew a lot about dread. It still surprised him though. All the different ways it could take over his body. This dread felt like someone squeezing that dangly piece of skin in the back of his throat.

"Wiley!" Principal V was waiting outside the smoky glass door for him. Chad was next to him, wide-eyed and pale. He was wearing a green T-shirt with "You Say Mommy, I Say Zombie" stretched across the chest. "Walk faster!" Principal V barked. Leo quickened his pace and slid just behind Chad.

Principal V leaned down so the boys' heads were within inches of his white teeth and flickery tongue. "Because of your incredible disrespect, your reckless behavior, your disastrously bad judgment . . ." With every word, the boys blinked back a spray of spittle. "I sentence you to one hundred hours of hard labor!" The mushroom-headed principal stood up and took in a shuddery breath. "To be performed in my office starting immediately!"

Principal V whipped two hula rags off his belt and presented one to each of the boys. He pushed them into his unicorned office. Then with one raised finger, he shouted, "DUST!"

ı ▸ ◥▬◣ ▴ ▸

"Um, excuse me?" Leo said. A fifth grader was standing in front of the 800s shelf. She was staring at a white unicorn in her open hand. "Um, are you dusting in this area?" Leo asked.

"Uuuuuuunnnnnh," she said, curling up her top lip.

"No problemo. Lots of room for unicorn dusters!" Leo said, making a wide circle around her.

Mrs. Bird, Chad's science teacher, was standing by the 200s shelf. She stared sadly at a green unicorn with red marble eyeballs.

"Mrs. Bird, are you okay?" Chad asked. "Shouldn't you be, um, teaching your students or something?"

"P-p-p-p-p-p." Mrs. Bird came at Chad, bubbles frothing on her lips.

"Ahhhh!" Chad yelled.

"QUIET!" Principal V's voice boomed from the hallway.

Chad shot Leo a look. There must have been half a dozen zombies "dusting" unicorns in Principal V's office. What was that about?

But Leo wasn't looking. He was waving his arms in an attempt to reach something high above the 1200s shelf. Something bright green, and not at all pointy, in a corner behind a silver unicorn with black teeth. What was that? Were those leaves? It looked familiar. Leo checked for Principal V's shadow outside the door. Nothing. He grabbed a stool from the corner and climbed up for a closer look. All of sudden, a hundred hours of hard labor seemed a lot more interesting.

5

ZOMBIFIED

"I have a theory," Leo said. Six hours of dusting down, Chad and Leo were back in Leo's lab with Roger. "Evil Principal V really *is* evil."

"Like, make-zombie-slaves-to-dust-your-miniature-unicorns evil?" Chad asked.

"Exactly," Leo said. "And I think he's using this plant to do it." Leo held out the sample of the bright green plant he'd taken from Principal V's office. "It's obviously some kind of cold-climate plant," Leo said. "Notice the fine silky hairs on the leaves. That's to trap heat. I *know* this plant," Leo said. "I've read about it. But I don't remember where or why."

"If *you've* read about it, it definitely has something to do with zombies," Chad said. "As in, it probably turns people into zombies."

"That's what I figured," Leo said. "But I can't find any record of it. Plus," he added after a pause, "I took a bite of it."

"You *what*?" Chad said.

"Many great scientists have been forced to use themselves as subjects," Leo said. "Right, Roger?"

But Roger was looking even more zombie-like than usual as he stared at the plant. "Such an odd color," he said slowly. "And notice the fine green powder at the base of the leaf."

"What?" Leo held the plant up to the light. "I don't see any powder."

"Here." Roger took the plant and turned it upside down to show him a small leaf near the stem. "It's just a few grains on the underside of the leaf. Easy to miss under normal circumstances, and this specimen has been tampered with. As you can see, someone has carefully wiped off most of the powder."

Leo jumped up and grabbed the plant from Roger.

"Don't even *think* about eating that powder, Leo!" Chad shouted.

"I'm not going to *eat* it," Leo said. He was so excited his voice squeaked a little. "I'm going to *examine* it."

He dipped a long Q-tip into the powder and wiped a green smear on a small rectangle of glass. Then he carefully placed another piece of glass on top of that one. "Microscope sandwich!" he declared, sliding the glass under a microscope. "Yeeeessssssssss!" Leo hissed as he squinted into the eyepiece. He stepped aside to let Roger take a look.

"My word!" Roger exclaimed.

"What? What is it?" Chad asked, taking a turn. "All I see are a bunch of lumpy green blobs."

"Exactly, m'boy," Roger said. "The bacteria known as Z. coli."

Leo added, "One of the most powerful zombifiers in the world."

Prioritize. That was the word Mrs. Chandler, Leo's English teacher, was always using. "What are your most important tasks?" he could hear her ask. "Identify those and perform them first." For once, Leo was glad he'd listened in class. He made a list of what he needed to do, most important tasks first:

1. *Stop Principal V from making more zombies.*

2. *Find antidote to cure zombies already made.*

Then he made more notes under his first task:

1. *Where is Principal V's Z. coli supply? (Find and destroy.)*

2. *How is Principal V spreading Z. coli to students?*

It didn't take a genius zombie scientist to figure out the answer to the last question. School lunch the next day was pizza, Rotfield Middle School's most popular entrée. That afternoon, the number of zombies at school went way up. Principal V's office was now crowded with moaning green zombies, dusting rags in hand. Chad and Leo had to push the undead away as they frantically searched for the Z. coli powder. But all they found was row after row of miniature unicorns.

"It's time to move on to step two," Leo told Roger and Chad that afternoon back at the lab. "There are too many of them. Our best hope now is an antidote."

"I've already been working on it," Roger said. "I've examined our plant from every possible angle. But I'm afraid I've reached an impasse." Roger sighed heavily and plopped down on his favorite hazardous materials box.

"That means he's stuck," Leo explained to Chad.

"My dear fellows, I need a specimen to test," Roger said.

"He needs a zombie to experiment on," Leo continued. After a pause, he added, "And I'm going to be it. Roger, pass me the Z. coli."

"No way!" Chad yelled. "We need your brain *alive* to help us out of this mess. If anyone's going to become a zombie around here, it's *me*." Chad poked himself in the chest, pushing in the *B* on his T-shirt that said, "My Other Body Is a Zombie."

"Well, my noble friends," Roger said, "I would volunteer, but I'm afraid that would complicate the results. Shall we flip a coin?"

"Wait. Maybe we could take a zombie from school?" Chad said hopefully.

"You mean *kidnap* a kid from school?" Leo said. "And have parents come looking? No way! Look, I live here already. It makes the most sense—"

UUUUhhhhhhhhhhhnnnnnnnn.

"Did you hear that?" Chad whispered. The boys shot to their feet and stood behind Leo's closet door. They heard heavy footsteps, and then—

CRAAAAAAAAAASH!

Leo pushed the door open. There was Shelly, sprawled out on the floor of his room.

One of her legs was bent weirdly around his desk chair. She was clawing the air in front of her in slow motion.

"*Aaaaaaaaaaaah!*" Shelly moaned.

"Shelly!" Leo said, running to her. "*You* ate the pizza?" She'd never touched a bite of school food in her life.

But as Leo walked closer to his sister, he noticed something that made him catch his breath. The dread grip in his throat tightened so fast that he gagged.

"Oh, Shelly," he whispered.

The sleeve of her blue T-shirt had been ripped off. Instead, oozing strips of skin hung down to her elbow. Blood streaked down her arm and onto her hands. There, between two lines of blood, was a sight that confirmed the worst: teeth marks.

CHAPTER

6

GREEN GLORY

"That means the zombies have started biting," Leo said. He was panting a little now. "The Z. coli will spread even faster. We need the antidote *now*." He placed both hands defiantly on his hips. "I'm turning into a zombie right this minute!"

Leo bolted for the lab, but Chad grabbed him by the back of his pants. "Think, Leo," Chad said, dropping his friend on the floor. Chad nodded toward Shelly and waited for Leo to catch on.

Leo sat stunned for a second before Chad's message sunk in. Of course. His stepsister, Shelly. She was a ready-made zombie specimen.

"MMMMMMnnnnnnn," Shelly moaned, now nibbling on the inside of her elbow.

"I'm sorry, Shell," Leo whispered. If he could, he would have hugged her to show her how much he meant it. Instead, he stuffed her mouth with the cleanest pair of socks he could find. Certain that she couldn't bite him, he circled duct tape around her wrist. Then he kept on circling the tape around the leg of a lab bench. It was official: He'd taken his zombie stepsister prisoner for the sake of medical research.

Leo and Chad had a full night's work ahead of them. First thing was making sure no parents messed things up. That was easy in Chad's case. He called his mother to inform her that he was spending the night at Leo's. As usual, she just said, "Un-huh, un-huh." And Leo and Shelly's parents had some ballroom dance contest that would last well past "bedtime."

Leo, Chad, and Roger worked late into the night. They tried extra-strength antibiotics, then laser therapy. They performed infrared shock, intestinal readjustment, and cardio echolocation. Now Roger was cradling Shelly's head in one arm. He spooned a yellow liquid into her gaping mouth. "Buttercup nectar," he explained.

"What about Principal V's plant?" Leo asked. He was online, scrolling through a site called 101 Zombie Home Remedies. "Do you have any idea what it could be yet?"

"Sadly, I do not," said Roger. He picked up the sample from Principal V's plant. "So strangely green," he said, twirling it in the four fingers of his right hand. "Green like—" Roger stood up at almost human speed. "*Mucinus maximus!*" He grabbed the jar with the slug and held it next to the plant.

"The exact same shade of green," Leo said slowly.

"Very curious." Roger reached for Leo's open laptop. His face became even greener as he opened the screen in front of him. "Very curious indeed."

<hr/>

At 5:02 a.m., Leo's eyes popped open. He found himself lying on top of a pile of dusty ferns. He must have fallen asleep while conducting the mucus extraction. Chad's head was nestled in Leo's right armpit.

"Ugh." Leo shot up and pushed Chad off and into a stand of crashing beakers.

"I'm up! I'm up!" Chad shouted, sitting upright.

Leo sat up too and rubbed his eyes. Then Chad rubbed his eyes. Then they rubbed them again.

Chad and Leo had seen a lot of surprises the past few days. But what they saw now topped the list. Shelly and Roger were sitting on Roger's box, heads together. They were looking at something on Roger's laptop.

"Leo!" Shelly jumped up and ran to hug her stepbrother. "Oh, Leo." She took a step back to look at him.

"Are you okay?" Leo asked. "I've been really worried about you."

"*You've* been worried about *me* for a change?" Shelly laughed. "I'm more than okay. Roger's found the antidote!"

"I guess so!" Leo said, grinning with relief. Not only was Shelly back to being human, but she also seemed cool about the half-zombie he kept hidden in a secret lab behind the back wall of his closet.

"Roger is simply a genius," Shelly said, wrapping her arms around him. Roger coughed a little, and his face turned greenish pink. "I can't believe you've been keeping him from me all this time." She squeezed Roger, and green pus oozed out of his left ear.

"I've been learning how Roger saved my life." Shelly turned the laptop around to show Chad and Leo a Web site called The Nordic Museum of Zombie Folklore and Fact. "*Nordic* refers to people who lived in northern Europe a thousand years ago," Shelly explained. She scrolled down to a section titled "The Outbreak of 982."

She read aloud: "For many years, experts have disagreed on this important event in zombie history. Is it just a myth, or did it really take place? Nordic records tell a spellbinding tale of zombie-like creatures walking the earth. The creatures are mysteriously returned to human form. The Torr Tapestry—"

"That's a rug with pictures on it, right?" Chad asked. He and Leo were both fully awake now.

Shelly nodded. "The Torr Tapestry tells the story in vivid pictures. Most interesting are the middle panels, which feature a curiously bright green plant. Experts have now identified this plant as the *Gloria viridis*, or green glory. Nordic peoples believed it held magical powers. Sadly, this fascinating plant is now almost extinct."

"That's it! That's the plant from Principal V's office! The green glory!" Leo shouted.

"It is, my friend! And look closely at this picture in the tapestry." Roger clicked to another page. Chad and Leo peered at the screen.

"That's our plant all right," Leo said. "But it seems to be covered in some kind of unripe berry or—" Leo squinted.

"They're slugs," Shelly said, "matching green slugs!"

Camouflage. The word popped into Leo's brain. The slugs were the same color as the plant because the slugs lived on the plant. They hid from predators by blending in with the plant's leaves.

Roger flinched as Shelly patted him on the back. "Rogie over here studied the entire tapestry for hours. He noticed that some pictures showed the green glory *with* slugs, and some showed the green glory *without* slugs. In the slug-off pictures, the people looked like zombies. In the slug-on pictures, they were human. And *that's* because the slug—"

"—is a *parasite!*" Leo finished. Answers were flashing like neon signs in his brain now. The slug lived off the plant. It didn't eat the plant's leaves—none of the leaves on the sample were chewed. It ate the green dust, the dust with Z. coli, the zombifier.

"Even more," Shelly was still going. "The slug gives off tons of mucus, or slime. That's why Roger first confused it with the North American *Mucinus maximus*." She pointed to the bright green slug. It was now in a jar with Principal V's plant instead of Roger's finger. "Of course, that's totally understandable. But the slime of this slug—the European *Mucinus sanitas*—is a powerful antidote to Z. coli. That was Roger's theory, and—" She held out her arms and twirled around. "I'm living proof that he was right."

"Whoa." Chad was resting his chin thoughtfully on one hand. "So let me get this straight. Principal V gets his hands on this rare European plant. He takes all the slugs off it, cuz they eat the zombifier in the plant's dust. He uses the dust to turn the whole school into zombie slaves. And now we need to cure everybody with the slug's magical slime?"

"Something like that." Shelly picked at a fingernail.

"Um, do we have any more slugs?" Chad asked.

"Sadly, no," Shelly said. "We're guessing Principal V got rid of the slugs. Except for one, obviously, which escaped."

"And I found," said Leo, "when I was swimming in gym last week. It had crawled under my green towel, probably looking for a habitat."

"I've got a plan! I've got it! Ding, ding, ding!" Shelly shot up and started dancing around like a game show contestant. "Notebook please, Leo!"

Shelly turned to a fresh page and outlined her idea in neat handwriting. Even Leo had to admit it was workable. And it got him to come up with a few good ideas of his own. After several minutes and just a few cross-outs, Leo and Shelly had done it. They'd mapped out a plan to save their whole school from zombiehood using just one slug.

CHAPTER

7

ZOMBIE MAYHEM

C had was in charge of weapons and armor. "We don't want to hurt the zombies," Chad stressed. "But we need a way to beat them off if they attack." He grabbed a checklist and went to the supply closet. Before long, he was standing by a heap of stuff. "Time to suit up," he said.

Chad, Leo, and Shelly tugged on stiff leather pants and leather jackets in various sizes and colors. "Hard to bite through," Chad explained. Next came the beekeeper hats. These were long white hoods with mesh covering the faces. Chad showed Shelly how to tighten the tool belt around her waist. It was for holding the weapons—a spray bottle filled with red liquid and a sock filled with marbles.

"Spray the tomato juice in their eyes to confuse them," Chad explained. "That will buy you a second. And the sock is actually far more powerful than a baseball bat."

"Hold this with your left hand," Chad continued. He handed Shelly the metal top of a trash can. "It's your shield."

"So this is it," she said, holding the lid out in front of her. "Got the slug, Leo?"

He patted his right jacket pocket. He wanted to say, "All zipped in," but his mouth could only make a dry, sticky sound. Today's dread felt like a monkey throwing rocks inside his stomach.

"You look absurd," Roger said, as the three zombie catchers turned to leave. "I mean that in the very best sense, of course." Roger smiled slightly. "Good-bye and good luck, my dear brave friends."

* * *

"It looks just like in the movies," Shelly whispered as Rotfield Middle School came into view. Zombies were everywhere. They drifted over the baseball field. They dragged themselves under the basketball hoops and around the playground. One zombie kept walking into the bottom of the slide over and over again.

"Okay, time for step one," Shelly whispered.

Chad put his arms out in front of him and made his eyes go blank. "Aaaaaaaaah," he moaned. Then, "How's that?"

"Perfect. Can you keep that up all the way to the swimming pool?" Shelly asked.

"Whatever happens, *don't run*," Leo reminded him, "and be as quiet as possible. As long as they believe we're zombies, they won't attack us." Then Leo slumped his shoulders and started dragging his left leg sideways across the ground.

"Nice touch, Leo," Shelly whispered.

Maybe it was easier to pass as a zombie with a pretend monkey banging inside your gut.

"Good luck." Shelly squeezed Leo's hand. "Now on to step two," she said. With a wave, she took off for the construction site across the street.

Slowly, slowly, Chad and Leo made their way into the zombie swarm. They passed Josiah Sullivan, then Molly Fisher, then Maddie Lee. There was Mrs. Chandler, chewing on home plate. "Guess class is cancelled," Chad whispered.

Leo and Chad were across the baseball diamond now. Past the dugout, an eighth grader in baggy pants appeared suddenly in front of Leo. She leaned in and sniffed Leo's neck like it was a steak on the grill. Leo jumped back just as her jaws snapped where his throat had been.

PPPPffffft. A spray of tomato juice covered her face, and she started spinning slowly in circles.

"Thanks, Chad," Leo mouthed.

Chad! Leo made a frantic circle with his finger to tell Chad to look behind him. Jeremy Berry was raking his fingernails across the back of Chad's leather jacket.

"AAAAAahhhhh!" Mouth open, Jeremy leaned in for a bite.

Whhhhaaaack! Without turning around, Chad swung his sock weapon up and back with a quick flick of the wrist. It bounced off the back of Jeremy's head. Jeremy stumbled just long enough for Chad to turn around.

"AAAAAAAAAAHA!"

This time Jeremy lunged at Chad full force. But Chad pushed him off with his trash can lid. Jeremy fell on his back like an overturned bug, and Leo quickly sprayed him with tomato juice. Jeremy's body went limp as he smacked his own face with one hand.

"They're catching on to us," Leo whispered, panic rising in his throat. He turned to see a dozen or so zombies slowly coming at them.

"Come on," Chad said. He pulled Leo inside the P.E. equipment shed and closed the door. "We'll lie low here, and they'll forget about us in a minute."

That was one good thing about zombies. They weren't very smart. And really not that strong either. A few zombies were no problem, but the whole school? Leo peeked out the window of the shed. Moaning, drooling, oozing zombies everywhere. And, wait a minute—

"Chad!" Leo called his friend over. "Look over there, on the swings!"

There, spinning a few feet off the ground, was the unmistakable mushroom head of Principal V. He was lying facedown over a swing, slowly twirling and untwirling the swing's chains.

That clinched it. Leo and Chad were the only humans at school today. *Good,* Leo thought, with a small wave of relief. For their plan to work, they needed to be the only living flesh around.

8

ZOMBIE FIELD DAY

"All clear for step three," Leo said. He and Chad were standing on the cement edge of the outdoor swimming pool. They had made it out of the P.E. shed and past the basketball hoops without any battles. In the distance, Leo could see Shelly in position. "On your mark, get set—"

"YOOO-HOOOOOOO," Chad yelled. "Here, zombies-zombies-zombies! Come on, you undead freaks! Fresh meat, oh yeah." He squeezed a roll of belly fat between his hands. "HHHHHAAAA-HAAAAA!"

"Yeah, you heard him, zombies," Leo shouted. "Fresh meat!" He jumped up and down and waved his arms.

"Who wants a bite of delicious Chad sushi?" Chad yelled. "Today's special? Butt roll!" he roared, wiggling his backside.

Chad slammed a couple of trash can lids together like cymbals and started marching around the pool. Leo stomped loudly behind him.

The plan was working. Zombies were coming toward them from every direction. They streamed out of the school doors and from the baseball field, the playground, and the basketball court.

"Oh yeah, come to papa," Chad said.

The zombies made a wide circle around the pool. As Chad banged and Leo stomped, the circle became crowded. The hungry zombies moaned louder and rocked harder. They closed in on Chad and Leo.

"Step four!" Leo yelled.

"Whoooooo-hooooo!" Chad shouted.

The two friends jumped into the pool with a giant splash. Quickly, Leo released the bright green slug from the sandwich bag inside his pocket. He turned the bag inside out and swished it under the water to get out all the slime. A light green circle rippled out around the slug. Leo and Chad gently waved their arms to spread the slime across the surface of the water.

For a second the zombies just stood on the edge of the pool. Then, *Splash! Plop! Splash! Ker-plunk!* One by one, the zombies fell into the pool. They came from all sides, pushing each other in like dominoes.

Leo squeezed his eyes shut. This was it, the moment of truth. When he opened his eyes again, the first thing Leo saw was Chad's grinning face. And behind that, the confused faces of his fellow Rotfield Middle School students.

"What's going on?"

"How did I get here?"

"I'm freeeeeezing."

"Hey, no splashing!"

Then came Shelly, right on time for step five. She rumbled toward them in a bright yellow bulldozer. She was carefully rolling a group of zombies along the ground with the front shovel. She stopped and turned off the engine at the pool's edge.

"Got all the stragglers," she called out. "But what do you want to do with *him*?" She pointed at Principal V. He was trying to crawl out from under her pile of dazed zombies.

Hmmm. Which was better? An evil genius principal or a deadly zombie principal? Deadly zombie, no doubt. But Principal V still had important information they needed. Plus, saving his life was probably the right thing to do.

"Throw him in," Leo called out.

"Okay, boss," Shelly said. And with the pull of a lever, she dumped the final five zombies into the giant pool of antidote.

EPILOGUE

L ike most evil geniuses, Principal V turned out to be a chicken. Especially when you knew what his weak spot was. All they had to do was hold a baseball bat over a glass unicorn. Sure enough, Principal V told them where the Z. coli was right away. The next day, Principal V's office was completely cleared out, down to unicorn 8,762.

Most kids had only fuzzy memories of being zombies. All they really remembered was the whole school splashing together in the pool. (Though Jeremy Berry developed an "inexplicable" fear of unicorns.) Two months later, the yearbook would show a picture of five hundred kids playing Marco Polo in the green water. "Best field day ever!" the caption read.

Leo and Shelly's parents had come in first place at the ballroom dance contest. They'd celebrated all night and slept in half the next day.

"Everything go okay at school today?" Mrs. Wiley asked Shelly and Leo that evening at dinner.

"Oh yes," Shelly said, shooting Leo a look.

"Definitely," Leo added. He liked the new feeling of sharing a secret with his big sister, Shelly Wiley, ZombieZapper #2.

Read each title in ZOMBIE ZAPPERS

ZOMBIE CAMP
ZOMBIE ZAPPERS BOOK 1

Get to know Zombie Zappers Leo, Chad, and the rest of the gang as they try to solve the mystery of the Smellerd zombies at summer camp. What nightmarish surprise will they find waiting for them at Lake Moan?

ISBN: 978-1-62285-003-7

ZOMBIE FIELD DAY
ZOMBIE ZAPPERS BOOK 2

Join the Zombie Zappers back at school for the next round of zombie mayhem. When Rotfield Middle School students start turning into zombies, Leo and his friends are the only ones who might be able to save them. Can they discover the cause of this outbreak before it's too late?

ISBN: 978-1-62285-005-1

THE ZOMBIE NEXT DOOR
ZOMBIE ZAPPERS BOOK 3

What if your next-door neighbor were a zombie? The Zombie Zappers return to find out exactly why Leo's neighbor is acting so strange in this suspenseful book. Leo learns a valuable lesson in the process.

ISBN: 978-1-62285-010-5

DOWN, ZOMBIE, DOWN!
ZOMBIE ZAPPERS BOOK 4

The Zombie Zappers jump back into action when a unique zombie outbreak spreads to their hometown. Leo will have to join forces with Chad's new best friend if they want to stop Rotfield from being overrun by a new breed of zombie.

ISBN: 978-1-62285-015-0